DEC 28 2021

Published in 2021 by Groundwood Books / House of Anansi Press
groundwoodbooks.com

Groundwood Books respectfully acknowledges that the land on which
we operate is the Traditional Territory of many Nations, including
the Anishinabeg, the Wendat and the Haudenosaunee. It is also the
Treaty Lands of the Mississaugas of the Credit.

We gratefully acknowledge for their financial support of our
publishing program the Canada Council for the Arts, the Ontario Arts
Council and the Government of Canada.

Canada Council   Conseil des Arts
for the Arts   du Canada

ONTARIO ARTS COUNCIL
CONSEIL DES ARTS DE L'ONTARIO
an Ontario government agency
un organisme du gouvernement de l'Ontario

With the participation of the Government of Canada
Avec la participation du gouvernement du Canada | Canadä

Library and Archives Canada Cataloguing in Publication
Title: Two at the top : a shared dream of Everest / words by Uma
Krishnaswami ; pictures by Christopher Corr.
Names: Krishnaswami, Uma, author. | Corr, Christopher, illustrator.
Identifiers: Canadiana (print) 2020039844X | Canadiana (ebook)
20200398547 | ISBN 9781773062662 (hardcover) | ISBN
9781773066226 (EPUB) | ISBN 9781773064208 (Kindle)
Subjects: LCSH: Tenzing Norkey, 1914-1986—Juvenile fiction. |
LCSH: Hillary, Edmund, 1919-2008—Juvenile fiction. | LCSH:
Everest, Mount (China and Nepal) Juvenile fiction. | LCSH:
Mountaineering—Everest, Mount (China and Nepal)—Juvenile fiction.
Classification: LCC PZ7.K75 Tw 2021 | DDC j813/.54—dc23

The illustrations were created in gouache on a smooth hot-press
Fabriano paper.
Design by Michael Solomon
Printed and bound in South Korea

For Leda Schubert
and Julie Larios, with
gratitude — UK

To Matthew, who took
me to the mountains
in the land of Edmund
Hillary — CC

TWO AT THE TOP
A SHARED DREAM OF EVEREST

Words by Uma Krishnaswami
Pictures by Christopher Corr

 GROUNDWOOD BOOKS
HOUSE OF ANANSI PRESS
TORONTO / BERKELEY

My name is Tenzing Norgay.

My name is Edmund Hillary.

When I was a child,
a boy like other Sherpa boys in Nepal,
I herded our yaks up the steep slopes,
to the edge of the rocks, where no grass grew.

When I was a child,
a scrawny kid in New Zealand,
I tended my father's bees.

I climbed higher and higher
to where the air thinned and I could see
the mountain, cloaked in clouds …

… Chomolungma, named for
a goddess,
touching the sky.

While other children played,
I dreamed of climbing all
the way up to the
mountain's
crown.

I walked half a mile to school,
barefoot in frost or fine weather.

I took long walks
and cut across the paddocks,
jumping over fences
with a stick in my hand,
my mind far away,
dreaming of adventure.

I was hungry for the snow-flecked peaks,
wind-whipped, ice-bound.
I didn't know how,
but I knew that one day
I'd climb to the very top.

My family laughed — what wild ideas!

I was sixteen when I saw
my first mountain,
Ruapehu,
on New Zealand's North Island.
When I climbed it, it took hold of me.

My brother sometimes climbed with me,
but I was the one who was wild
about mountains.

Running away to the city,
I hired myself out to carry loads
for the foreign climbers
flocking to Nepal's high ranges.

Slowly, slowly,
carrying loaded packs on my back,
climbing many mountains,
I grew stronger.
My dream became a vision.

When war broke out, I joined the air force.
At training camp, I spent weekends climbing
mountains near the military base.
Shipped out to the Pacific front, I saw
the war end, before a boating accident
sent me home again
to the peaks I loved.

Once more, I took care of my father's bees,
and every chance I got,
I climbed.

Sacred to my people,
the mountains were my friends.

Open crevasses,
rumbling avalanches,

glowing, blue-green
glaciers ...
I came to know
them all.

I tramped up every mountain I could,
in New Zealand and Australia.

When my parents traveled to Europe,
I went with them, but I went climbing.
Five peaks in the Swiss Alps — in five days!

Six times, then seven,
I climbed Chomolungma —
the English call it Everest —
but never to the top.

Not yet.

I joined Himalayan climbers — even tried Everest, but didn't make it to the top.

Not yet.

Now here we are, in 1953.
We have made our way
up icefalls, over glaciers,
battling winds that roar
like a thousand tigers.

Now we have been
climbing Everest
for eighty days,
crawling on rope bridges,
hacking footholds with ice picks.

In the murky dawn,
we have only a thousand feet to go.

Onward,
cutting steps into the ice,
blinded by sunlight on snow,
up a crevasse whose edges
slip and shift with every heartbeat,

listening, listening

Up a steep ridge,
then sliding down, down,
groping for a foothold,
struggling back up again.

for the roar of the next avalanche.

Test the ropes.
Jam the ice-axe
into the crevice.

Secure the lines.
Up and up,
and there it is,
a rounded snowy dome.

Ice everywhere!

We haul ourselves
between rock and ice.

A few more whacks of the ice-axe
in the firm snow ...

And here we stand at the top
of Chomolungma.
"*Thuji chey*" — that is how we say it
in Sherpa. "I am grateful."

Here we are,
at the top of the world,
at the summit
of Mount Everest.

Imagine Mount Everest

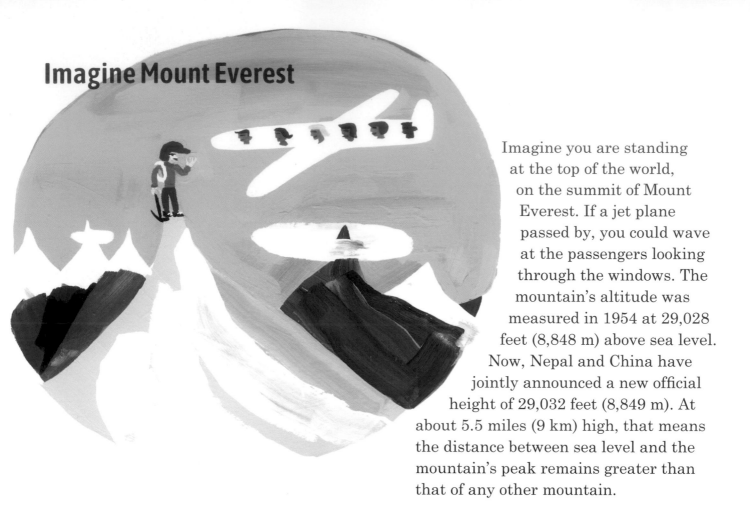

Imagine you are standing at the top of the world, on the summit of Mount Everest. If a jet plane passed by, you could wave at the passengers looking through the windows. The mountain's altitude was measured in 1954 at 29,028 feet (8,848 m) above sea level. Now, Nepal and China have jointly announced a new official height of 29,032 feet (8,849 m). At about 5.5 miles (9 km) high, that means the distance between sea level and the mountain's peak remains greater than that of any other mountain.

29,032 feet
(8,849 m)
above sea level

The Earth is not a perfect sphere (its diameter is greatest at the equator). Because of this, Chimborazo, a mountain in Ecuador, is 3,967 miles (6,384 km) above the Earth's center — about 1.2 miles (2 km) farther above than Mount Everest. Still, Everest remains the mountain with the greatest height measured from sea level to peak.

Mount Everest stands on the border between two countries, Nepal and China, in the mountain range called the Himalaya. Ten of the world's fourteen tallest peaks are in these mountains. The range was formed about forty-five million years ago by the northward drift of the Indian subcontinent, pushing the land that was once at the bottom of the sea up against the rest of Asia, causing it to fold into giant peaks.

There are other ways to measure a mountain's height. Nearly 33,500 feet (10,211 m) from base to summit, Mauna Kea, on the island of Hawaii, is taller than Mount Everest — but much of it is under water. With 13,796 feet (4,205 m) of the mountain rising above sea level, Mauna Kea's altitude is lower than Everest's.

The mountain is named for George Everest, the leader of a massive project to measure and map India. Begun in 1802, the Great Trigonometrical Survey of India took over sixty years to complete. It established Mount Everest as Earth's highest mountain above sea level.

Tenzing Norgay and Edmund Hillary were not alone on their famous expedition. The team, over 400 strong, was led by mountaineer John Hunt and included 362 porters, 20 Sherpa guides and close to 10,000 pounds (4,536 kg) of baggage.

Hillary and Norgay remained in touch off and on throughout their lives, becoming not just mountaineering teammates but good friends. In 1960, Hillary founded the Himalayan Trust, an organization dedicated to improving the education and health of people in the remote Everest region.

Since Norgay and Hillary first reached the summit in 1953, more than four thousand people have finished the climb. Many others try and fail. Some die trying. A famous British climber, George Mallory, was asked why he wanted so badly to climb the mountain. He said, "Because it is there." Mallory died in his last attempt in 1924, probably without getting to the top.

Today, hundreds of people climb Mount Everest each year. Thousands more hike to the base camp at the foot of the mountain. Is that too many people? Who will clean the trash they leave behind on once-pristine slopes?

The Khumbu region of Nepal, where the mountain is located, is home to Sherpa people like Tenzing Norgay. Their

In the sky, bar-headed geese fly over and through the massive ranges, at altitudes deadly to trained mountaineers.

But the perfectly evolved cycles of life on the mountain slopes are changing. Glaciers usually melt slowly in the summer. They feed mountain streams and rivers, making life possible for thousands of miles around. Yet for the last 150 years, the Earth has been getting warmer. Climate change, caused by burning fossil fuels, by pumping too much carbon dioxide into the atmosphere, is melting the glaciers too quickly.

Most of the world's nations have agreed to work together to limit climate change, even as scientists warn us that time is running out. Humanity's great challenge is to find ways to protect the snowy world over which Mount Everest looms.

villages, connected by steep paths, teeter on ridges and dot the lower slopes of the mountain. Stone arches and rows of prayer wheels welcome travelers. Rounded stupas or chortens, topped with small spires, symbolize the Buddha. Suspension bridges sway across rivers and streams. Waterfalls roar. In a short growing season, villagers harvest barley, cabbage and root vegetables from tiny terraced plots. Buddhist monks live and pray in monasteries filled with ancient statues and paintings.

Far across the rocky terrain, snow leopards roam, hunt and raise their young. The lower reaches of the mountain are home to blue sheep, red pandas, black bears, wild goats and gray wolves.

Note: This story is an account of historical events, told through the literary device of imagined first-person voices.

Selected Sources

Dhital, Megh Raj. *Geology of the Nepal Himalaya: Regional Perspective of the Classic Collided Orogen*. New York: Springer, 2015.

Hillary, Edmund. "The Summit." Chapter 16 in *The Ascent of Everest* by John Hunt. London: Hodder and Stoughton, 1953.

Hillary, Edmund. *View from the Summit*. New York: Simon & Schuster, 2000.

Keay, John. *The Great Arc: The Dramatic Tale of How India Was Mapped and Everest Was Named*. London: HarperCollins, 2000.

Norgay, Jamling Tenzing with Broughton Coburn. *Touching My Father's Soul: A Sherpa's Journey to the Top of Everest*. New York: HarperCollins, 2001.

Norgay, Tenzing with James Ramsey Ullman. *Tiger of the Snows: The Autobiography of Tenzing of Everest*. New York: G.P. Putnam's Sons, 1955.

Tenzing, Judy and Tashi. *Tenzing and the Sherpas of Everest*. Sydney: HarperCollins, 2010. Ebook.

Source Notes

"A few more whacks … firm snow." Edmund Hillary, "The Summit." Chapter 16 in *The Ascent of Everest* by John Hunt (London: Hodder and Stoughton, 1953), p. 205.

"'*Thuji chey*' — that is how we say it in Sherpa. 'I am grateful.'" Tenzing Norgay with James Ramsey Ullman. *Tiger of the Snows: The Autobiography of Tenzing of Everest* (New York: G.P. Putnam's Sons, 1955), p. 4.

"Because it is there." In "Hazards of the Alps," *New York Times*, 29 August 1923.

Comparable Books for Young Readers

Burleigh, Robert. *Tiger of the Snows: Tenzing Norgay: The Boy Whose Dream Was Everest*. Illustrated by Ed Young. New York: Atheneum, 2006.

Francis, Sangma. *Everest*. Illustrated by Lisk Feng. London: Flying Eye Books, 2018.

Jenkins, Steve. *The Top of the World: Climbing Mount Everest*. Boston: Houghton Mifflin, 1999.

Stewart, Alexandra. *Everest: The Remarkable Story of Edmund Hillary and Tenzing Norgay*. Illustrated by Joe Todd-Stanton. London: Bloomsbury Publishing, 2019.